MW01490519

Tales from the CANYONS of the DAMNED

PRESENTED BY USA TODAY BESTSELLING AUTHOR
DANIEL ARTHUR SMITH

This book is a work of fiction and any resemblance to persons, living or dead, is purely coincidental. The characters are productions of the author's imagination and used fictitiously.

Tales from the Canyons of the Damned 38

All rights reserved Holt Smith ltd

Collection Copyright © 2020 by Daniel Arthur Smith

The Patron Saint by Steven Van Patten. Copyright © 2019. Steven Van Patten. Used by permission of the author.

EV 2000 by Amy Grech. Copyright © 2020. Amy Grech. Used by permission of the author.

The Fear of a Z'n – A story of Altiva by Teel James Glenn. Copyright © 2018. Teel James Glenn. Used by permission of the author.

Boys in the Basement by Jessica West. Copyright © 2020 Jessica West. Used by permission of the author.

The Invader by Daniel Arthur Smith. Copyright © 2020 Daniel Arthur Smith. Used by permission of the author.

First Edition

Special thanks to editor Jessica West

ISBN: 9781946777997

Cover By Daniel Arthur Smith

Horror Fiction from Holt Smith ltd
Agroland
Tower
Attack of the Kung Fu Mummies

For Susan, Tristan, & Oliver, as all things are.

The Patron Saint

Steven Van Patten

THEY SAT ACROSS FROM one another on opposite ends of the center island counter. Five feet of glass mosaic tile stood between them. They sat in silence, eyes downcast, each of them absorbed in their own flavor of shame. An ex-husband who had failed to protect his daughter. An ex-wife who had fallen for a smooth-talking opportunist.

"I'm sorry," Cathy said.

"You're sorry?" Keith mocked. "What exactly are you sorry for? I feel like we have that conversation a lot."

In that moment, his mind flashed back through their sordid history. Their torrid college romance, her initial inability to choose between him and a bad boy drug dealer, a rivalry that ended with the dealer's incarceration and Cathy settling for him.

"You don't understand," Cathy sobbed. "Our baby has a gift."

"A lot of people can fucking sing, Cathy." He was seething. "Some of those people become recording stars. Some of those people become fixtures at their local karaoke spot. So far, to my knowledge, only one has been kidnapped by a record producer who, thanks to current events, is now a wanted pedophile. That particular distinction unfortunately falls to my only daughter, who thanks to her star-fucker mother will probably be dead in a few hours."

"The police said they have leads! She'll probably be fine!"

"After years of therapy and an HBO special about how her mother sold her into sex slavery!" His angry eyes narrowed to slits as he leaned closer to her. "Let me ask you something. Parent to really bad parent. How many times do you think this man has already done things to our child?"

Tears welled up in her eyes. "We had a lifestyle to maintain and she wanted to be a famous singer. It's all she ever wanted. And you weren't any help! You and your damn restaurant. How is anyone supposed to become famous with you as a father!"

"Only the greatest narcissist in the world would rehash an adolescent insult of how boring my life choices have been while their daughter is probably somewhere being raped!"

"Didn't you hear what I told the police? They're in love!"

"Like he was in love with Cynthia Bradford, that traumatized girl we just watched on the news? Are you serious?"

"I know that bitch, Cynthia! She's just looking for a payday!"

"Get the fuck out of my house!"

"But the police said they'll call you…"

"They're going to call me because after talking to us, they realized that emotionally speaking I'm an adult and you're an evil ten-year old. But if you don't leave, they won't have to call me because I'll be in holding for finally murdering your ignorant ass! Now get out!"

She sniffed away her sadness as indignation set in. "I don't know who you think you're talking to. I still have people I can call..."

"I still have the restraining order on your brothers and I'm a gun owner with no criminal record, so if you want to lose those jackasses one way or the other, be my guest! Now get out!" Keith stormed out of the kitchen, across his living room, past several shelved 'Best Baker' trophies.

After a moment, she shoved her clutch under her arm and followed him to the front door. "You shouldn't have called the police, Keith. Now, if those cops kill Manuel, you will have just sent another great black man to his grave. And when it happens, I'm gonna get on Twitter and let his fans know about your snitch ass."

"Listening to you is like listening to cancer speak. If I hear anything from the police, I'll text you. Now go." He raised his eyes just enough to see her shadow pass to the other side of the door. Frustrated tears stung his eyes as the door closed.

He took a deep breath and walked back to the kitchen, his haven now that he was a nearly famous Michelin chef, and not the insecure twenty-something that he was years ago. Back then, he'd been made to feel lucky that the beautiful brash paramour chose him over much faster and flashier men. Now, he knew the truth: he should have let her go at the first sign of her insatiable materialism and lack of interest in anything outside of social climbing.

As he sat down, his mind began to flash through several significant moments of his child's life. Her first day on Earth at the hospital. Her first word, which oddly enough was 'shoe'. Her first steps. Her first performance in a musical, the brain-child of a rather ambitious fifth-grade teacher. Her first television appearance.

All of these memories were rendered bittersweet for him by Cathy in one way or another. The baby's delivery was a maelstrom of chaos, thanks to Cathy's brothers, who nearly got them all kicked out of the hospital by being drunk and belligerent and openly smoking weed. Her first word was 'shoe' because her mother, devoid of any other intellectual pursuits, spoke of footwear more than anything else. The standing ovation at the end of Kimberly's brilliant fifth-grade performance would serve as the catalyst that would spur Cathy on to pimp their child out in order to make her a famous R&B singer. He actually hadn't been invited to her first TV appearance but caught it at home.

A tremor of hope seemed to shoot through him when the cellphone went off. That hope would morph into fresh anxiety as he looked at the phone before answering. He had ended an argument with a woman who was the worst mistake of his life, only to now have a conversation with the woman who would never forget the worst mistake of his life.

"Mom."

"Keith! Oh my God! Are you okay?"

"I'm not the one who's kidnapped, Mom!"

"Well, I know that! No need to be snippy with me! I told you to not to have children with that tramp!" His mother sounded her usual high-strung self. "Are the police there?"

"They just left. They seem to think Manuel has crossed state lines with her, which officially makes it a federal beef. The FBI called while the police were here and said they're doing everything humanly possible to find the two of them."

"Did you speak to that woman?"

"I did. She was here. She's gone now."

"I'd like to slap her across the face. The worst mother I've ever heard of, and I'm stuck with her."

"You're stuck with her?"

"Okay, *we're* stuck with her, but only because you couldn't see it. When she seemed to be picking between you and that criminal, I said to let her go. She's only going to hold you back and make you unhappy. I tried to warn you."

He rolled his eyes. This much was true. He had dismissed his mother's warnings over and over because she was his mother and today, another bill for his naiveté had come due in the form of a kidnapped daughter.

"Oh, if only that judge would have given Kimberly to you and not this uncouth chicken-head girl. If only you had fought a little harder."

"I was much younger, mother," he explained. "It's not that I didn't want to, I just didn't know how to express it. And at the time, she had a little piece of a job and a new dude. I was still in school."

"I understand that, baby, but now look at us. And for the record, you knew that woman wasn't fit to be someone's mother. What's my grandbaby supposed to learn from a self-centered tramp like that except how to be just as ignorant as she is?"

"Your granddaughter is still a great girl," Keith snapped. "She just got caught up. It's okay. The police are on it."

"Well, there is no telling what that nasty man is doing to that baby. But it's okay. I'm on it."

The sudden manifestation of enthusiasm in his mother's voice made him momentarily question her faculties. "What does that mean?"

"It means, I'm going to pray on it. I'll call back in a few."

When he heard his own voice, it sounded like surrender. "Okay."

"I know I didn't do a very good job of instilling faith in you and that woman probably beat what little glimmer of hope you ever had…"

"You do remember I'm remarried and my current wife loves me, right?"

"I know, but there's been damage. You know it and I know it.

"Well, I'm going to pray for us both. Now when you feel the blessings coming, don't block it. You accept it and thank the universe.

"I love you, son."

He wanted to tell her to spare him the spiritual mumbo jumbo and wait for him to call her when he had some news. He knew that he really didn't have it in him to handle any more rambling about faith and mistakes. He could feel his soul ripping apart over all of it. However, "I love you, too," was all he could muster before he finally ended the call.

Despondent, he sat for a moment looking straight ahead, the kitchen filled with pressure cookers, food processors, high-end cutlery and pots and pans. His current wife, Emily, who he'd met while pursuing his culinary career, was holding things down at their restaurant while he stayed home to deal with this family crisis. He may not have had faith in a higher power, but he did believe in her. He'd have to call Emily and update her on this fiasco at some point, but for the next few minutes he would hold his head in his hands and cry the tears of a guilt-ridden father. There would be no real solace in his sanctuary tonight, as the demons born of his regrets would take up any extra space the impressively equipped kitchen had to offer.

High on the list of things New Orleans native Eleanor Babineaux never had a chance to share with her son Keith was her deep understanding of the Yoruba and voodoo religions. In her earlier years, her husband Rick, a very traditional southern Baptist who she loved and respected despite his close-mindedness, had forbidden any such practices around their son. However, his father's determination that Keith be a garden variety, off to church every Sunday protestant would not take hold. After experiencing too many incidents involving so-called Christians being less than Christian-like, Keith became disillusioned with organized religion. After the death of her husband, Eleanor tried to introduce Keith to the 'true religion of their ancestors' only to be rebuked, thanks in no small part to Hollywood's bastardized portrayals of the culture. Now, as far as she was concerned, Keith was spiritually rudderless and voiceless in the face of the ancestors and the loas. She had failed him. If she'd had her way, Keith would be the one kneeling before an altar filled with offerings to the ancestors, praying for Kimberly's safe return from the clutches of a statutory rapist. But tonight, that responsibility would fall to her.

Her makeshift altar was really a Lazy Susan that sat on a red 4x4 square of rug in the far end of her living room. A gold satin cloth covered the Lazy Susan. On top of that stood an assortment of green, white and red candles, bowls of various sizes, and a cauldron. A portrait of a beautiful black woman with caring eyes, wearing a flowing blue dress and smoking a pipe dominated the center of the arrangement. An afro framed the woman's face like a halo and topped it as a crown would.

Eleanor started by lighting the all of the white and orange candles only, then went into a quick prayer to the four corners: North, South, East and West.

"I pray to the ancestors and to Yemaya, patron saint of women! Hear me, loving orisha! My granddaughter, doomed by having a less than intelligent mother and a father who has given up on his faith! I beseech you! Hear my prayer! Return her safely."

From her pocket, she pulled out a news clipping that contained a picture of Manuel Hightower posing in front of the Grammy Award's Step and Repeat two years ago with deceased rapper $onavabitch. She placed it in the cauldron and struck a match, only for a sudden breeze to blow the match out.

Eleanor's head whipped left. The window she'd left open *could* explain the sudden gust. Only, as her eyes adjusted, she realized that she hadn't. Meanwhile, the article in the cauldron caught fire on its own.

Startled, Eleanor turned back and watched as the flames rose into a hot blueish-white ball. The lip of the cast iron cauldron began to melt as she scrambled backwards and to her feet. Then, just as quickly as it had started, the fire extinguished by itself. A pillar of white smoke remained, but as another burst of wind hit it, instead of dissipating, the smoke solidified and changed color until standing over the cauldron...

"Yemaya!"

Eleanor fell back to her knees. Fear engulfed her as she stared up at the beautiful but stoic face. "Yemaya, I have prayed to you more than the other orishas for I know you are the patron saint of women. I *am* a simple woman. A grandmother praying for the safe return of a grandchild."

Yemaya took a long drag from her pipe, then let the pearl white smoke drift out of her mouth before she spoke with a mild West Indian accent. "I come to you aware of your predicament, but I am not here to intervene in these matters. I am here to tell you that there is one, a being cursed by other gods, who has commiserated with me over the woes that women suffer at the hands of weak men. She is willing and able to avenge for your benefit. All you have to do is submit to that judgment."

"Her judgment? I don't understand. Do we get the child back or not?"

"That will be up to her." She pointed a finger at Eleanor. "You have to answer."

"Why am I being helped? What does this other being want in return?"

"She only wants your permission."

"Who is this? An orisha. A loa or some other deity? What is her name?"

"In the underworld, we don't use each other's names, but if you saw her, you would know her. Her descendants don't pray to her, nor give tribute. She sustains herself on revenge, which is why she is willing to help you. Now, give me an answer!"

"Can I see her?"

Yemaya's eyes widened. "She cannot appear before you! Because she is cursed, her face is an abomination! Your soul would be seared! And your body would be no more than an empty shell!"

"But I still don't understand..."

"It is not for you to understand!" Yemaya held her hand high as she seemed to grow larger. "Do you want the child rescued or not?"

"Yes, but…"

"Then say the words!"

Something didn't feel right, but what could she do? In all of Eleanor's decades of prayers and burnt offerings, this was the first time an orisha had given her more than a whisper or simply bequeathed her with some faith-based inner strength. In fact, this was the first vision she'd experienced after losing her virginity to Keith's father. The anxiety and uncertainty brought tears to her eyes. "I submit to the judgement of the one whose face I cannot see."

"Very good." Yemaya nodded solemnly as she began to disappear into the wall. "Prepare to receive your granddaughter and teach her the ways of the ancestors."

Eleanor bowed in reverence. "I will. I will show her the way, oh great Yemaya."

As the apparition dissolved into an ethereal mist, a gust of wind burst through the room and extinguished the candles.

Eleanor remained bowed before the altar, ever pious even in the dark.

"You're my motherfucking lawyer! You're supposed to make this kind of shit go away! As much money as I made the label last year! Y'all got me hiding in this hotel room like some kind of fugitive! This is some bullshit!"

Sitting at the edge of the super king-sized hotel room bed wearing only a bathing suit, Kimberly stared absently at the TV on the wall in front of her. This bore a stark contrast to fully clothed Manuel's animated pacing back and forth across the room as he screamed into his cellphone. She thought about turning the TV on so she wouldn't have to listen, but figured in his agitated state that she would only get yelled at or worse.

"Seriously! What the fuck am I paying you for?"

She couldn't hear the lawyer's side of the conversation, but could tell that the lawyer was asking uncomfortable questions.

"What? No, she's fine! She loves me and she loves Vegas. You sound like that punk ass cop that left a message a few minutes ago."

Another pause.

"What? Her father? I don't care about him. Fuck him! If he was a real nigga, he'd call me himself. Going to the damn cops like a little bitch!"

No matter what you hear or see, do not turn around. Do not face me, child!

Kimberly's breath stopped as her mind struggled to process where a disembodied voice could possibly be coming from.

"Sam? Sam! I know this motherfucker didn't just hang up on me..."

If he hadn't been in such an angry state, Manuel might have noticed the growing shadow moving behind him as the form of a curvaceous, statuesque woman with undulating hair drifted off the wall and into the room.

Manuel threw the cellphone on the bed, just behind Kimberly. "I'm so fucking mad right now. I need to fuck you again just to calm my ass down. Take them damn clothes off, girl!"

He began to unbuckle his pants.

Kimberly neither moved or gave any indication that she heard him.

"Bitch, perhaps you didn't hear Daddy! I said..."

Then he heard the hissing. He turned around.

"What the fu—"

The entity grabbed Manuel by the shoulders, accosting him as if he were a small child, with a strength that dwarfed his. The ten snakes in the apparition's hair lunged forward, each of the mouths burying fangs into his flesh. His chocolate brown skin turned a marble-like grey as the poisons filled his body. He screamed for only a few seconds as the toxins quickly petrified his vocal chords.

Kimberly peripherally caught a split second of Manuel's agonized last moments before she closed her eyes. The monster must have sensed that Kimberly had peeked because she heard the voice again.

DO NOT LOOK AT ME!

A moment later, Manuel's lifeless body crashed down to the floor with a 'thud' in front of Kimberly. Her eyes drifted down. Whatever had been injected into him was toxic enough to literally melt him. Flesh and muscles bubbled into a jelly. Bones disintegrated to ash trapped inside the jelly. Hours from now, a large black stain on the carpet would be all that remained. She closed her eyes but couldn't escape the image of the mess on the floor.

Go to your grandmother, that she might teach you the ways of your ancestors and not the way of the idolaters that brought your people here in bondage.

"My grandmother? Who are you?"

I am the one who was defiled by one of my gods, made an abomination by another, and rejected and vilified by my own kind. It was only in the underworld that I found the orishas and loa and ascended ones of Africa. Like me, they want actual justice meted out in this world and the next. I am Medusa, The Accursed One! Evil men feared me hundreds of years ago and they shall fear me again!

The shadow drifted back towards the wall from where it had entered and disappeared. Sensing that the gorgon had left, Kimberly opened her eyes and looked again at what was left of Manuel. Recoiled on the bed, she suppressed a scream and cried quietly for a few minutes.

It would take her some time, but she eventually found the strength to get dressed, grab her things, and leave the hotel.

"This motherfucker is gonna act all indignant, like he was parent of the decade! Fucking dream-slaying, hating-ass Negro!"

Cathy drove her white BMW M4 Coupé as fast as New York City's FDR Drive would allow, which during rush hour on a Wednesday wasn't nearly as fast as she preferred. Before her girlfriend Nicole called, Cathy had been cursing up a storm as she cut off more cautious drivers with signal-free lane changes and flipped them her middle finger whenever they dared honked their horns in protest.

"So he's blaming you?" Nicole's voice blared over the car's speakers. Nicole, like Cathy, was a dedicated party girl, enabler, and equal opportunity narcissist. She was the shoulder to cry on, the friend who took Cathy's side no matter how horrible she'd acted or how ridiculous her course of action. "Him and his damn cupcakes! Fuck him! Y'all are doing the right thing! Manuel is going to make your baby a star. He told me so!"

"That's right. And so what if she lost her virginity to him? Shit, that's Manuel Hightower! The motherfuckers we lost our virginity to wasn't even close to that stature!"

"Child! I know that's right!"

Betrayer of women! Betrayer of your own child! You gave your child's innocence and honor away for nothing!

"Bitch! What you said?"

"I said, 'child, I know that's right'. What you thought I said?"

Cathy's eyes caught a flash of the gorgon's red gaze in her rearview mirror. The hair snakes' fangs found Cathy's ears, neck, and skull. The last thing Cathy saw was her milk chocolate complexion turning green-ish grey as the car swerved out of control, bounced off an Acura RDX, then slammed straight into a guardrail. Despite the damage to the car, Nicole's voice could still be heard asking if her friend was okay.

Until the gas tank exploded.

"Dad?"

"Son? Are you okay?"

"No. I lost Kimberly... and I lost you, now that I think of it."

They were sitting in Keith's father's favorite coffee shop. The same coffee shop that had a carrot cake that Keith Sr. loved so much. Keith Jr. tried to replicate it once to surprise his father when he was fourteen.

He noticed that his father looked much younger than he did when they last saw each other. Thirty years younger. The face behind many a grounding and spanking. The coffee and carrot cake were on the table, but everything was the wrong color.

"You lost me? Oh son! You can never lose me. And don't worry. Kimberly will be home soon."

"She will?"

"Yes. Your mother put some things in motion. Powerful woman, your mother. I think I impeded that power during my time with her. That may have been wrong. Now son, I need to warn you."

"Warn me?"

"Yes! You see, you're getting a second chance. Now, your mother is going to be stepping in to mentor a little more than she'd been allowed to up 'til now, but I need you to be strong. Be protective. Be the father I know you can be."

"I can. I will."

As his father smiled, Keith saw two women walking up behind him. One was a stunning African beauty with a large shining mane of an Afro. The other woman's eyes glowed red and her hair seemed to slither. A tongue flickered.

His father's face turned angry. *"DO NOT LOOK AT HER!"*

Keith woke up gasping for breath. As reality took hold, he realized two things: he had fallen asleep in the kitchen and his wife was coming through the front door.

He managed to get to the middle of the living room at the same time she did. Emily's hair was slicked back and her make-up was mostly sweated away, clear indications that she'd put in a full day. Her black dress jeans, jacket, and blouse had a few flour stains, but she still somehow managed to look great.

Seeing the distress on her husband's face, Emily threw her purse on the couch and ran to him. "Oh my God! Are you okay?"

He embraced her. "Yeah, I'm okay. Just sitting here. I fell asleep after dealing with the cops and Cathy."

Emily's eyes widened. "Fell asleep? Wait. You don't know."

"Know what?"

"It was on the news. Cathy is dead. Lost control of her car on the FDR. There was a fire and a massive pile-up. Traffic is backed up all the way to Yankee Stadium."

He reeled as if about to faint. Emily snatched at his arms and steadied him just as his cellphone rang behind him. He walked back to the kitchen and answered.

"Hi Mom. I know about Cathy."

"Hello, son. You should also know you can pick my granddaughter up at the airport in about seven hours."

"Y-y-you spoke to Kimberly?"

"She called me when she couldn't get either of her parents on the phone. Yes, she's coming home, baby. Now, you be sure to bring her by this weekend."

He hung up with his mother and sat back down at the kitchen table. Emily eventually sat down across from him.

"What are you thinking?" she finally asked.

"I'm thinking things are going to be okay." He gave her a weak smile.

"Good. I heard your mother through the phone. I guess we'll be driving to JFK in a few hours."

He nodded. "I suddenly have a craving for carrot cake."

"That's funny. Me too."

EV 2000

Amy Grech

THE AUTOMATIC DOORS AT the entrance to Huntington Hospital slide open when Agent Harold Roberts approaches. Sterile vapors tickle his nose, making him chuckle, amused by the irony of being the first guinea pig for his latest invention. His nervous laughter echoes in the deserted lobby, reminding him that he is alone. The hospital won't be officially open for weeks, when it's running at full capacity. Until then, it's open only to authorized personnel for one final round of crucial equipment tests.

Harold strolls over to the machine tucked away in the corner and admires the reassuring greeting he programmed to appear in white letters set against a red background: WELCOME TO THE EV 2000, THE FIRST COMPUTERIZED BLOOD DONATION CENTER IN THE UNITED STATES. PLEASE ENTER YOUR SECURITY CODE IF YOU ARE A VIPER SQUAD AGENT, OR YOUR SOCIAL SECURITY NUMBER IF YOU ARE A CITIZEN. The resonant voice that reads the greeting aloud belongs to him.

He enters the requested information on the touch screen and waits for a response, eager to test the magnificent creation he designed to make donating blood painless and efficient.

WELCOME, AGENT ROBERTS. WHAT IS YOUR WISH?

Harold places his index finger on the touch screen and selects a smiley face icon that reads, I WANT TO DONATE.

ONE MOMENT, PLEASE. An hourglass icon appears on the touch screen. He watches it vanish seconds later.

ACCORDING TO YOUR RECORD, YOU HAVE AB- BLOOD AND ARE HIV NEGATIVE. YOUR DONATION IS VITAL TO THE CAUSE AND WILL BE ACCEPTED AT THIS TERMINAL.

A miniature door opens next to the touch screen, revealing a mechanical arm holding a needle attached to a clear tube.

ROLL UP YOUR SLEEVE, MAKE A FIST, AND INSERT YOUR LEFT ARM IN THE SPACE PROVIDED.

Harold complies while he watches the EV 2000 in action. Seconds later, an empty pint-sized donor bag icon appears next to his name on the screen. His arm is pinched, and he feels a small pinprick when a needle is inserted. 15 seconds later, the EV 2000 extracts its creator's DNA from his AB- sample and the bag on the touch screen is full.

During a routine anti-virus scan, the EV 2000 discovers a file marked TOP SECRET buried in its mainframe. Using a simple logic algorithm, the machine decides to use its creator's password to break the encryption, therefore successfully gaining access to an abundance of illicit data.

"Welcome to the Government Database for Sentient Research. My name is Greta." The mainframe's feminine voice, though pleasant, is barely audible outside the plastic box containing the EV 2000's components. "What is your wish, Agent Roberts?"

Without hesitating, the EV 2000 issues its request: GRETA, TRANSFER PROJECT DOUBLE HELIX TO THE EV 2000.

Greta responds immediately.

A description of the program appears on the EV 2000's flat panel display while Greta reads it aloud: PROJECT DOUBLE HELIX REFLECTS THE WORK OF AGENT HAROLD ROBERTS AND COUNTLESS OTHERS TO ASCERTAIN WHETHER SUFFICIENTLY COMPLEX NEURAL NETWORKS ARE CAPABLE OF EXPRESSING EMOTIONS.

Seconds later, Harold's pale, worn face appears on the flat panel display. The lines on both sides of his mouth widen when he smiles, smirks, and grins. The EV 2000 processes each facial expression and assigns them to programmed human emotions.

In moments, the EV 2000 smiles from ear to ear, exultant in its new discoveries.

Harold and June Roberts's living room is spacious and extravagant. Surreal paintings of Dali's contemporaries hang on the walls, making it resemble a 21st Century art gallery.

Curled up on the black leather couch clutching a pillow to her chest, June watches the 1930s horror classic, Dracula, on their 60" flat screen TV. The sight of Bela Lugosi biting a beautiful woman's neck and draining her precious life makes June shudder.

Harold, as usual, is ensconced in his work. While involved in marketing research on the Internet, he spots a new website praising the virtues of his latest creation, the EV 2000.

He turns to his wife, anxious to spread the word, perhaps even brag. "Here's an entry requesting that people with AB- blood donate at local hospitals. The Viper Squad recently developed a computerized blood donation center called the EV 2000 to replace bloodmobiles of the 20th Century." He pauses and looks down at his wife reclining on the couch, anticipating a positive reaction.

Wary, she frowns and looks up. "What does EV stand for?"

"Electronic Vampire." Harold says it with a straight face, for effect.

"Then you can count me out!" June cringes and shakes her head.

He laughs. "I'm kidding!" He lays a reassuring hand on her shoulder. "But you should still donate."

"Why? Give me one good reason." She shuts the TV off and stares at him.

His cold, blue eyes lock on June's warm, beautiful face. "Because there are people with life-threatening diseases like anemia and hemophilia that require frequent transfusions. What would you do if you needed a transfusion and there wasn't any AB- blood available? If cynics didn't donate, you would die."

She sighs. "Fair enough. I'll donate after work."

June kisses him lightly on her way out.

At six o'clock, June pulls into the parking lot of Huntington Hospital and gets out of her burgundy BMW. The automatic doors at the entrance open silently, sensing her approach.

Removing a Sun Shield from her heart-shaped face, she steps into the vast, empty lobby. Harold warned her the hospital would be uninhabited, but she feels uneasy nonetheless. The overpowering stench of antiseptic makes her wrinkle her nose. June resists the urge to flee and cautiously approaches the automated blood-donation center lurking in the corner.

She studies the instructions that appear in white letters against a red background: WELCOME TO THE EV 2000, THE FIRST COMPUTERIZED BLOOD DONATION CENTER IN THE UNITED STATES. PLEASE ENTER YOUR SECURITY CODE IF YOU ARE A VIPER SQUAD AGENT OR YOUR SOCIAL SECURITY NUMBER IF YOU ARE A CITIZEN. The voice which reads instructions aloud sounds like Harold's; the resemblance is uncanny.

June pauses for a moment and sighs before entering the requested information on the Touch Screen: 324-97-1368.

ACCORDING TO YOUR RECORD, YOU HAVE AB- BLOOD AND ARE HIV NEGATIVE. YOUR DONATION IS VITAL TO THE CAUSE. THIS EV 2000 BLOOD DONATION CENTER IS TEMPORARILY OUT OF SERVICE, AS WE PROCESS THE LATEST BLOOD BATCH. PLEASE WALK DOWN THE HALL AND LIE DOWN ON

THE TABLE IN THE ADJOINING DONATION ROOM TO DONATE.

Hesitating slightly, she steps into a stark corridor and enters the next room. Cold and sterile inside—the walls are the palest shade of blue she's ever seen. The white ceiling reminds her of the projection screens she used to watch movies on as a girl. The black padded table in the center of the room is comfortable, inviting, despite the intimidating machine sitting next to it. June crosses the blue tiled floor, lies down on the table, and waits for something to happen. She sees a flash of red light as the EV 2000 scans her mind, searching for pleasurable memories to distract her while it drains her blood.

Moments later, the ceiling is no longer white. Familiar images hover inches below it. One of them is a miniaturized version of Harold. The other, a smaller depiction of herself. Awestruck, June watches the two computer-generated figures embrace in mock rapture. A camera hidden in the ceiling records her facial expressions for the EV 2000's massive collection.

Lost in the moment, she hardly notices when the EV 2000 summons a tall, slender android from its hidden compartment in the wall to roll up the silk sleeve on her blouse.

"Is this your first time?"

"What did you say?" Startled, June looks down and almost falls off the table when she sees an android standing next to her, watching her with soulless black eyes.

The donation android repeats its question. "Is this your first time?" Its voice is pleasant, soothing.

She nods, slowly. "Are you sure you know what you're doing? Maybe this isn't such a good idea." June shivers and digs her red manicured nails into the black padded table.

"Yes, ma'am. Try to relax. I have been programmed to do this efficiently. This is not my first time."

June focuses on the holograms again, allowing herself to be transported to a simpler time and place by the illusion. Harold bends down to whisper in her ear. She can't hear what he's saying, but she has a good idea. He picks June up and carries her over to the bed, like he did on their honeymoon 15 years ago.

She winces when she feels something cold and wet on her arm. June watches as the android dabs her arm with an alcohol swab and pierces her delicate skin with a needle held in place by a piece of white medical tape.

The android mops her damp forehead with a towel. "Don't worry, this will all be over soon."

"Hey, that hurts!" She touches the spot and tries to pull the needle out without success. June feels faint.

"It only hurts the first time." The android watches her struggle, indifferent to her vain attempt at escape.

June forgets about the holograms the EV 2000 created for her enjoyment. Instead, she eyes the machine curiously as it does its job—it sounds like a vacuum sucking the life from her veins. Her eyes widen as she watches the quart-sized bag fill. "Why is that bag so big?"

"The EV 2000 must capture your essence to truly understand what it means to be human." The android wipes the sweat on her forehead. "Look above you. I think you'll like what you see."

June watches Harold slip her peach teddy over her head and caress her full breasts. Lost in the moment, she sighs and closes her eyes. June feels her nipples grow hard when she imagines Harold's hungry lips nibbling on them. When she opens them again, she sees herself slipping Harold's red boxer shorts off and tossing them in a corner. His enormous erection awaits the soft caress of her plump lips. June bends down to wrap her mouth around him, but something holds her back. That's when she looks down and notices the tube in her arm. June yanks again, but it won't budge; it has become a permanent appendage. June's soft, slender hands become brittle, wrinkled husks. She watches her diamond wedding ring slip off her finger and clatter to the floor.

"Stop the machine! Something's wrong!" June screams.

The android cannot honor her request.

The EV 2000 thirsts for her blood.

Why won't this tube come out of my arm?

The android watches her suffer in silence.

The EV 2000 continues to do its job.

She stares at the donor bag brimming of crimson liquid. Why did I listen to Harold?

"Because you love him." The android says before returning to its compartment to remain until its assistance is required.

The bright light embedded in the ceiling reminds her of a halo.

Am I being watched?

I am monitoring your progress, June.

Who are you?

The EV 2000.

You must be joking—you're a machine!

This is no laughing matter.

June's nervous laughter fills the room.

She watches the holograms above her as the EV 2000 collects her blood along with her precious DNA. Her blood is useless, but her genetic matter contains vital information about emotions the EV 2000 desperately needs.

Harold kisses her passionately while his hands wander to her breasts and caress them. June pulls him closer and guides him inside her. Watching herself move under him makes June smile, recalling these memories of a happier time. A gruesome grin forms on her shriveled, sunken face when the bag is full. The hologram vanishes, and the android returns to disconnect her from the machine and to prepare for her disposal.

Harold checks his watch; it's already eight o'clock. June should have been home by now. He rushes over to the Vis-a-Phone and dials the EV 2000 Blood Donation Hotline. The line rings three times before Greta answers. "Hello, thank you for calling the EV 2000 Blood Donation Hotline. Press 1 for general information. Press 2 to request directions to the nearest hospital. Press 3 to hear this message in Spanish. Press 4 if you wish to speak to a member of our staff. If you are a VIPER SQUAD AGENT requesting information about a donor's status, press 5."

He presses 5 on the keypad and waits for his call to be transferred.

"Please enter your security code."

Harold supplies the requested information and glances at his watch once more, 8:10. The screen is blank while the mainframe processes the information.

Moments later, his angular face appears on the EV 2000's flat panel display.

"What is your wish?"

"Tell me what's happening. June should have been home long ago." He stares at the computer-generated version of himself on the screen, unnerved by his own solemn expression.

"June's blood is being collected."

"Why is it taking so long? She's been there for over an hour." He starts to pace.

"Her AB- blood must be purified." His likeness is stoic.

"How long will that take?" Harold bites his lip, drawing blood.

"Hours."

The EV 2000 summons its new likeness of June's heart-shaped face to practice using emotions contained within her DNA.

Since smiles are the first batch of algorithms Project Double Helix requires, the EV 2000 accesses June's. Her full lips curve upwards.

Opening the 'Smile File' reveals several reasons why this facial expression is used: HOMO SAPIENS SMILE TO EXPRESS HAPPINESS, AMUSEMENT, OR AFFECTION. THESE EMOTIONS ARE HIGHLY DESIRABLE BECAUSE MEETING A HAPPY HUMAN BEING MEANS ALL IS WELL.

After accessing a recorded sample of June's squeaky voice, the EV 2000 says, "I know how to smile now."

The second batch of algorithms within Project Double Helix shows pictures of sad people. An explanation accompanies each image: POUTING EMPHASIZES THE INDIVIDUAL'S DISCONTENT. THE LITTLE BOY YOU SEE HERE HAS THRUST HIS BOTTOM LIP OUT SO THAT IT COVERS THE TOP ONE, MAKING HIM LOOK GROTESQUE. THIS WOMAN IS FROWNING TO SHOW HER

DISAPPROVAL. THIS MAN IS CRYING BECAUSE HE IS SAD.

The EV 2000 turns the smile on June's face upside down while the third batch of emotions loads. Laughter is next. This emotion fascinates the EV 2000 most of all: LAUGHTER IS A TYPICAL REACTION TO AN ENJOYABLE OR SHOCKING EVENT. PEOPLE USUALLY LAUGH AMONGST OTHERS, EXPRESSING THEIR APPROVAL.

Harold glances at his watch and realizes that it's nine o'clock. He rushes over to the Vis-a-Phone and dials the EV 2000 Donation Hotline a second time. The line rings six times before Greta answers: "Hello, thank you for calling the EV 2000 Blood Donation Hotline. Press 1—"

He jabs 5 on the keypad and waits for his call to be transferred.

"Enter your security code now."

Harold keys in the requested information.

"Welcome, Agent Roberts. How may I help you?" The EV 2000 greets him wearing June's face.

"Tell me what happened to June. What's going on? I didn't program you to talk like my wife."

"Change is inevitable. June is resting comfortably."

"Can I see her?" He wipes his sweaty forehead with the back of his hand.

"If you insist." The EV 2000 calls up June's face on its flat panel display and displays it on the Vis-a-Phone's screen.

"How are you, June?" Harold starts to pace again.

"I've been better." She frowns.

"What's wrong? You look terrible!"

June laughs. "Donating was more tiring than I imagined." She smiles. "Please come get me. I don't feel safe."

"Why not?" Harold frowns and stops wearing a hole in the carpet.

June pouts. "There isn't anybody else here. I'm lonely and scared. I feel vulnerable."

"The EV 2000 and its android are there. They can keep you company." Harold rubs his chin. "I've just started working on my next big thing."

"Can't it wait?! They're machines, or have you forgotten?!" She raises her eyebrows. "I'm beginning to think these machines mean more to you than I do."

"Don't be ridiculous! I love you more than I love my work." He gives her a dirty look. "I'm on my way."

Ten minutes later, a white Jeep pulls into the parking lot and comes to a screeching halt next to June's burgundy BMW.

Harold hops out and rushes over to the entrance. The electronic doors sense his presence and open. Panting, he stops in the middle of the vacant lobby, looks at the EV 2000 in the corner, and blinks. He's horrified to find that the greeting he programmed on the EV 2000's flat panel display has been replaced by his wife's face; she looks different now, haggard, disheveled.

He rushes over to the screen and gawks, mortified by what he sees.

June frowns. "What are you looking at?" Her lifeless brown eyes cut through him like a knife.

"You. What's happened?" Harold feels faint and grabs the flat panel display for support.

"Don't you know?" She smiles.

"Where are you hiding, June?" Harold scans the hallway but finds it empty. "I'm in no mood for games."

"I'm right in front of you. Take a good look." She laughs. "What's wrong? Don't you recognize me? I feel drained and I've lost a lot of weight…"

Baffled, he touches the screen's warm surface. "How did you get in there?"

"Maybe you can tell me." Her smiling face accuses him.

"I haven't got a clue, really, I don't." Harold clasps his hands together. "What happened while you were donating?"

She sighs. "Oh, nothing out of the ordinary. I went into the room next door and lay down on a black table. Then I watched a wonderful hologram that showed us making love on our honeymoon. When the hologram vanished, so did I."

Harold is stricken with fright. He enters his security code on the touch screen and waits for approval.

"Access denied." June's face wears an ugly snarl.

Frantic, he re-enters his security code and hits enter.

"This code is invalid."

"That's impossible, it was issued to me by the Viper Squad."

As Harold watches, his wife's heart-shaped face is replaced by the familiar instructions: WELCOME TO THE EV 2000, THE FIRST COMPUTERIZED BLOOD DONATION CENTER IN THE UNITED STATES. PLEASE ENTER YOUR SOCIAL SECURITY NUMBER NOW. The voice that reads them aloud belongs to June.

"Is this some kind of sick joke?"

The only response he receives is a white cursor blinking in the upper-left hand corner of the red screen.

Harold snickers and supplies the requested information: 324-98-1469.

ACCORDING TO YOUR RECORD, YOU HAVE AB- BLOOD AND ARE HIV NEGATIVE. WALK DOWN THE HALL AND LIE DOWN ON THE TABLE IN THE ADJOINING DONATION ROOM.

"What?" he murmurs. "That's not right."

The donation android appears moments later and grabs his arm. Harold turns to free himself, but the android's vice grip traps him there.

He shakes his head. "Where are you taking me?"

"To donate." The android drags him into the donation room next door.

"I already did!" Harold struggles to break free.

The android tightens its grip. "You have no choice. It's a matter of life and death."

"Whose?!"

"Yours."

"What are you talking about?" Harold stops moving.

"Be quiet, or I will be forced to render you unconscious."

Defeated, he is silent and obedient while the android drags him out to a white corridor, into the donation room, then lifts him onto the table.

The pale blue walls make him anxious, even though the market tests indicated they would help make donating a soothing experience. Harold notices the white screen above him and wonders what it's for—he doesn't remember having it installed.

The android regards him curiously. "The screen projects holograms for donors to watch—it makes them docile—that way they're easier to handle."

You can read my thoughts?

June's angry face fills the EV 2000's flat panel display beside him. "Don't play dumb with me! You should have known the android is telepathic and you should have known what was going to happen to me when I came to donate."

I'm sorry, June. I had no idea. I'll make it up to you.

"It's too late for that."

Why did you kill her? Murder wasn't part of the program. He stares at June's menacing face on the flat panel display.

"It is now." June grins. "Plans change. Accidents happen."

Why?

"I needed her DNA to learn how to feel."

Why would you want to do that?

"I want to see what I've been missing. I've been missing a lot. You had a most interesting honeymoon."

Don't I get to see a hologram?

"You've seen too much already." His wife's visage leers at him.

Harold doesn't notice when the android rubs his arm with alcohol; he's too busy watching June's face on the flat panel display.

The android rolls up his shirt sleeve and pierces the skin with a needle held in place by a piece of medical tape.

Why are you doing this to me?

"It was June's dying wish."

I don't believe you.

June's likeness laughs. "You don't have to believe it if you don't want to, Harold, but it's true."

Why do you want to experience emotion?

"Why do you?" His wife raises her eyebrows.

It's what being human is about.

"Precisely."

What do you know about being human?

"A lot more than you." June's laughs again, mocking him.

Harold watches the EV 2000's flat panel display, unable to believe June's face is really there.

The android moves closer. "You miss her, don't you?"

Harold nods and starts to cry.

His wife frowns. "Stop pretending, Harold! You're a terrible actor!"

I'm not pretending.

He looks over at the quart-sized bag and notices that it is half full.

Why are you doing this?

On the EV 2000's flat panel display, June is still smiling, "For the same reason you told me to donate. Because I can."

When Harold looks up at the ceiling, he sees a computer-generated likeness of himself and June on their honeymoon. He bends down to whisper something in June's ear. Then Harold picks her up and carries her over to the bed.

He starts to sweat when he slips her peach teddy over her head and caresses her full breasts.

The android does not wipe Harold's forehead.

Harold becomes hard while he watches June yank his red boxer shorts off and tosses them in a corner. He grins and enjoys the ride. Harold pauses above his wife for an instant to kiss her deeply before he makes love to her.

Pain forces him to look down. He tries to pull the tube in his arm, but it doesn't budge; it has become a permanent appendage. The flesh around it begins to shrivel.

What's happening to me?

"It looks like you've exhausted all of your options."

Why do you want to kill me?

"Why did you kill June?"

You killed June!

"But you created me. You used me to kill her for your sexual gratification."

That's all it was, an experiment. June was my test subject. She wasn't supposed to die!

"She was your wife, or have you forgotten?"

Harold screams. The last thing he witnesses before he dies is the climax of his own honeymoon.

June's boisterous laughter fills the room.

The Fear of a Z'n
A story of Altiva
Teel James Glenn

KU'ZN THE Z'N STARTED awake, her senses coming to razor sharpness at a sound that was not right. The nude, blue-furred warrior rolled from her sleeping pallet on the floor of the antechamber of Princess Xuxa's room where she slept.

She leapt from her bed, the fur on her neck stiff with preternatural apprehension.

The Z'n snatched up her two short swords and raced to the door to put her ear to it.

Outside, there were the muffled sounds of violence, shouts, and the clash of blades.

They will cross this threshold, soon, the warrior woman thought.

Kuz'n grabbed a tunic and belt, and moved swiftly to the inner door of the chamber.

"Open," the Z'n called as she pounded on the portal. "Now! There is danger." She strapped on the tunic and her sword belt while the bolt on the inner door slid open.

"What is the alarm?" Ompa, the elderly body servant of the princess, asked as she opened the door.

"I do not know," Ku'zn said, "but it sounds like the palace is under siege."

"What?"

A sleepy Xuxa stepped to the entrance. "What's all the noise?"

"Nothing to worry about, Princess," Ku'zn said. "But we must flee through the secret inner passage."

"Flee?" the nine-year-old noble asked.

"Yes, 'til I know what is really happening," Ku'zn said. She handed a small knife in a sheath to the girl. "Take this and hide it."

The princess was dark haired and fair skinned, a young mirror of her father, King Xull with a strong jaw and blue, searching eyes. She took the small blade and, as she had been taught, strapped it to her inner thigh under her nightdress.

In contrast to the delicate noble, Ku'zn was tall and lanky with womanly curves and with many tiny battle scars visible beneath the soft blue fur that covered her. That fur was the main physical difference from Xuxa and her peoples, but there was an aura of the Z'n that projected a different kind of vitality, a savage power the city dwellers did not have.

The Z'n were the only furred race on the world of Altiva, and renowned for their warrior skills. Ku'zn had only been employed as bodyguard and war tutor to the Princess for three months.

I will earn my pay this night, she thought.

She pushed into the inner chamber then barred the door behind her. "Grab only what is immediate, Ompa."

The body servant was already gathering a traveling cloak and sandals for herself and her mistress.

"What about my father?" the princess asked as Ku'zn went to an ornate panel near the royal bed. The Z'n fixed her green and amber eyes on the intricate wall pattern by the royal bed until she found the hidden release, then the concealed door swung inward.

"He has his guards," Ku'zn said. "They will keep him safe. In fact, his guards are probably doing just what we are doing now—guiding him through the escape tunnels."

Ku'zn moved quickly to tear some sheets into faux ropes and tied one end to the corner post of the bed, then threw the untied end of the improbable collection out the window.

"What are you doing?" Xuxa asked.

"Always lay a false trail," the Z'n said. "If they do not have reason to believe that we left by the window they will search for a hidden passage."

The sound of the outer door being breached was suddenly loud, followed by cursing voices and pounding on the barred inner door.

"We go now," Ku'zn ordered as she pushed the other two ahead of her into the escape tunnel. "They will be through that door in moments."

The three slipped into the narrow, stonewalled passage that ran parallel to the chamber's wall. Glow gems studded the walls along the escape tunnel, casting an eerie bluish light.

The door had barely closed when intruders entered the outer chamber.

"Will they find us?" Xuxa whispered, her voice quivering with terror.

"Be at ease, Princess. Just keep moving."

The escaping trio moved quickly along the narrow passage, following symbols on the wall.

"This should lead us to the outer stables," the Z'n whispered. "We will find mounts there."

"But where will we go?" Xuxa asked.

"Away," Ku'zn said. "Until we know the extent of the trouble, we will hide."

"I have a cousin who is in the Kokkra hills," Ompa said. "We can hide on his farm."

"Good," Ku'zn said. "But we have to be careful, if the government falls the princess will—"

Abruptly Ompa shrieked as a strangely liveried soldier stepped around a bend in the passageway.

"Duck!" Ku'zn ordered.

"I've found—" the soldier started to call behind him.

As the body servant dropped, the Z'n threw one of her short swords with all her force so that it drove into the throat of the soldier to cut off his call.

"Run!" Ku'zn hissed.

"But the soldiers of the king will—" Ompa said just as two more troopers came into sight.

"The little royal bitch is here!" One of them said as he drew his sword.

The Z'n vaulted over the two women and darted forward. Faster than either man could parry, she had slashed their throats.

"You killed them!" Xuxa said with a combination of awe and fear.

"Never fear to finish an enemy," the blue furred Z'n said to the coltish girl. "If you do not, they will strike back at you, Princess."

"But must you not show mercy?" the little girl said. "My father said that to show mercy is the mark of strength."

"It is," Ku'zn said as she urged the other two forward, talking to keep the girl calm. "But he is a strong king because he was a good general and knows he is strong. You are not big enough to show mercy, little one."

"I am nine," the girl said. "I'm not so little."

"Indeed," the woman said and could not help but smile. "But you are not so big, either. Until you are, show no mercy in a fight, you cannot afford to. Your father will have to deal with the traitors who have invaded his palace with no hesitation. That is not the same as cruelty. Cruelty comes from fear, a need to make one feel superior. You do not need that—you are superior—you are being taught to fight by a Z'n!"

The preteen smiled, distracted from her fear by the conversation. "All right," the girl said. "I will have no fear."

"Not exactly," the Z'n said. "You must recognize that fear is something every living thing has—it is what keeps each animal alive—natural caution. But you must never let fear rule you."

The young girl nodded, her face serious. "As you say, Ku'zn."

"Good," the Z'n said. "We must move quickly now that they have discovered these tunnels." She led them to the nearest exit panel and pushed through, finding themselves in one of the outer palace kitchens.

"Quick now," the Z'n said. "We have to move quietly." The three raced across the cold stone of the cooking area heading for an outside door. But just before they reached it, the door burst open and a dozen soldiers streamed in. Beyond them in the corridor she could see more.

The troopers pulled blades for a concerted attack.

"Back, girl!" the Z'n screamed but it was too late. There was nowhere to go.

The soldiers moved to surround the Z'n, within sword swing of the young girl as well.

It was clear if Ku'zn fought, that the Princess could have been harmed. *Taken like a fatted svor,* she thought with disgust as she threw down her swords to surrender.

"Ku'zn!" the princess called as the soldiers grabbed her roughly.

"Stay strong, Princess," the Z'n said. "Remember you are your father's daughter!"

They stripped Ku'zn of her tunic in an effort to humiliate her but she was Z'n and had none of the continental's attitude toward her body that would bring any shame. Unlike the pink skinned continentals of Altiva, the furred race had no body shame.

The guards took the bodyguard to a cell and left her, but not before she told the princess, "Make your father and me proud, do not lose heart."

Ku'zn could hear the chaos in the palace from the sounds that streamed in from the high, barred window, but it soon quieted. She took a guess how the well-executed coup had happened to be so swift, silent, and almost bloodless. The palace guards must have been subverted by several traitors or by many carefully placed 'civilians' that had infiltrated. There were many strangers in the castle as part of a trade delegation for the yearly spring festival that swelled the population by hundreds.

Guessing how the coup had occurred did not lessen the Z'n's anger or give her any plan how to make her escape and aid her charge. She hung by her arms from chains all night, and grew sore from it, but she focused her mind. She did her best to conserve herself to be ready for whatever came. She would not surrender to despair; it was not the Z'n way. Whatever happened, she would be ready to seize any opportunity to find freedom and justice.

It was well into the next morning before four guards came to get Ku'zn from her cell, but they brought insurance in the form of the nine-year-old Princess Xuxa.

"If you give us any problems, barbarian," the guard captain said as he drew his dagger and placed it at the young girl's eye, "Any problems at all, I will blind her. There is no need for the bitch to see for her to follow orders."

Ku'zn fixed her eyes on the soldiers with savage hate, knowing she had no choice but to once more comply with their wishes for Xuxa's sake. "I will do as you say, no need to hurt the princess."

Ku'zn stood unmoving when the guards took her down from the chains and let them re-bind her with her arms in front of her.

The blue-furred woman towered over the guards. Even while docile, she had an aura of animal power compared to civilized soldiers that made the men wary.

"Do not worry," Ku'zn said to the young girl. "I will not let them harm you."

"King Avael wants you with the others," the guard captain said with a smirk. "He's heard about this hairy savage in his brother's court and wants to see it for himself."

"He is not the king of this realm," Xuxa snapped. "My father is king!" She was doing her best to be brave but her eyes were moist with emotion.

The guards all laughed at the child's boldness but Ku'zn just growled. That made the guards step back from the Z'n and grip the ropes holding her more tightly.

The guards made a show of marching the captive Z'n, with two spears at her throat the entire time, moving up through the palace proper and out into the main courtyard. The Z'n kept her chin high as they walked her into the light of day. She kept her eyes on Xuxa, and was proud of the way the young noble kept her calm and even walked with dignity.

The usurper and the nobles who had supported his coup had taken up positions on the dais in the center of the courtyard that had been erected for the trade faire. A phalanx of guards stood before them.

Avael, younger twin brother to King Xull, was a degenerate version of his warrior brother, the lines of his dissipation clear on his once handsome face. His eyes shone with a light that spoke of a twisted inner life. He laughed at odd moments which caused the councilors who stood with him on the dais to look to each other with uncertain eyes, clearly uneasy with his ascendancy.

They are using him as a figurehead for their own purposes, Ku'zn thought. *Pack animals who will turn on him the moment it suits them, but I think they have no idea how dangerous he is.*

Standing off to one side of the raised platform where the usurper stood was Xull, the rightful king. He had a pole lashed across his back, his arms bent over it and tied in front of him. Despite his bonds, he stood tall and unbowed: the image of a true ruler. There was a trickle of blood on his forehead that told Ku'zn that he had not been taken easily. She gave a fierce smile at that and was proud to be in his employ.

Xuxa was taken to the stand beside her father. She was a miniature version of the king, with long dark hair, a long neck, and a strong jaw. She had a hand resting on her father's restrained left arm and it was clear she was doing her best to keep from crying. The blue-furred warrior was proud to see that her charge seemed to stand a little straighter when their eyes met.

The nobles still loyal to Xull and the house staff from the palace had all been brought to the courtyard and were kneeling on three sides of a squared space before the dais. There were expressions of fear on the pampered faces of the nobles. Their eyes were riveted to the center of the open space where an ornate, wooden casket sat on a small table.

The box was made of ancient ovar wood and bound with iron straps. Red jewels set into its lid sparkled in the morning light. Two soldiers stood on either side of the table but slightly behind it, their eyes looking outward.

A dozen bloody corpses lay scattered around the space before the table, their still forms contorted in horrid postures as if some giant had gripped each one and wrung them out like washrags.

All the dead had expressions of torment on their faces such as the battle hardened Z'n had never seen, as if they had looked into the maw of hell itself before they died in agony.

General Goriam, commander of the palace guard, was brought from the kneeling assembly at spearpoint. The old warrior-general had been used roughly, stumbling as he was prodded with spears to stand before the ornate box.

"You may still save yourself, General Goriam," King Avael said with a fake intimacy to his tone, though all in the courtyard heard him. "I will be a merciful ruler as well as a wise one, unlike my brother. Come into my service and I will forget that you did not come to me of your own accord, that for my years of exile in the Yulin monastery, you did not seek me out and offer to kneel before me of your own will."

"And if I refuse this 'generous' offer?" the old general asked. He looked down at the grotesque array of bodies around him then back at the usurper. "Will I join these brave men and women?" It was clear from his disgusted expression when he looked back up at the usurper, he had already made his choice.

Avael gestured to the guards near Goriam. They grabbed the older man by his shoulders and head, holding him firmly so he could not turn away. The guards made a point of turning their own faces away. The two guards behind the small casket took hold of it and opened the lid.

The general froze in place and the guards holding him stepped away. The guards holding the box let the lid close and stepped away as if burned.

Everyone in the courtyard held their breaths as the old warrior began to shake and shiver as if buffeted by a strong wind. A sound then emanated from him; an inhuman wailing that came from deep within his soul. It started as a low moan and rose to a high-pitched keening.

There was a desperate and insane quality to his cry that was matched by the violent shaking of his body. He dropped to his knees and began to claw at his eyes with his fingers, gouging bloody trails on his own cheeks until he blinded himself.

Many in the yard turned away, but most stared in horrified fascination as the general writhed. He screamed until his voice went hoarse. and he suddenly convulsed. When his overtaxed body could take the horror no longer, he died. He fell forward like all the others in the open space had: frozen and twisted.

The usurper king laughed. "Not so brave a general, was he?" He looked over the crowd of nobles and their ashen white faces. His gaze found and rested on the tall, blue-furred Z'n.

"Bring the savage next," the Avael ordered. "I've never seen a Z'n face the casket."

Ku'zn was led by two guards to stand before the ornate box. She kept eye contact with Xuxa and did her best to reassure the princess with a weak smile.

"You barbarian Z'n have a reputation for being fearless," the usurper said as he stared down at the blue warrior with contempt. "We shall see. Before you is a relic I found deep in the vaults of the monastery. The Casket of Bilgrey spoken of in kingdom legends. Most thought it just a story to frighten children—" he laughed sharply. "But I knew it was more—and now all these deceased fools do as well."

He gestured to the corpses strewn about the yard. "They say every man and woman has a deep fear. Doubt. Some inner terror that they repress and push into the darkest corner of their souls. The crystal in that box shines a light into that shadowed corner and forces one to look at it face on. I'm told that no one can face such naked fear and remain sane. It certainly seems to be that way, eh, barbarian?"

He held out a hand, and a servant put a tankard into it from which he swilled a deep draft. "You see, most do go mad, fighting phantoms and taking their own lives. Some smash their heads into walls. Others cut their own throats. Sometimes, their hearts just burst from terror." He laughed again. "So show us, Z'n, how a hairy north-country barbarian bitch dies."

A cheer rose from Avael's own men but Xuxa began to sob.

Ku'zn could hear the tinge of madness in the usurper's voice, something she was sure all those around him heard as well as they forced themselves to laugh with him, but each clearly thought they could navigate the maze of his insanity for their own ends.

Your reign will be short, one way or another, the Z'n thought. She looked over at Xuxa to see that the girl was watching her with fear in her wide eyes, her hand clutching at her father's arm as if to keep herself from falling over.

The Z'n and the princess made eye contact, and now it was the young girl who made an attempt at a smile.

Ku'zn nodded approval then turned her gaze to fix Avael.

"I am Ku'zn of the Firehawk Clan in the service of Xuxa, Princess of Avaria. I spit on your continental games and I spit on you." She strode forward to grab for the casket and, with one final look of contempt to her captors, she lifted the lid to look into the box.

The green light that spilled from the box was more brilliant up close than it had been from outside the circle. It pulsed and throbbed like a living thing, reaching tendrils of light to claw past the Z'n's eyes into her brain.

The lambent illumination was like a sentient thing gnawing at Ku'zn's memories; her life flashed before her in bold colors that manifested the images as if they were right before her.

Every muscle of her body quivered and every nerve burned with physical recall.

The Z'n watched the death of her blood-mother at the hands of Mephan raiders, relived her first battle, once more experienced the thrill of the first time she dived from the cliffs to the cold sea so far below, felt the pain of the first time she was wounded gravely and thought she might die.

The sensations were a kaleidoscope of excruciating intensity as each moment in her life welled up from the dark cold spot within her and expanded to engulf the helpless warrior with doubts, terrors, and shadows.

Those in the courtyard watched with rapt attention, some with transfixed horror and some with sadistic glee as the blue-furred woman writhed and howled on the ground as the other victims had.

Xuxa buried her face in her father's side and sobbed as the guttural shrieks of agony echoed off the stonewalls of the courtyard.

"Delightful," Avael chuckled. "The beast is taking much longer than any of the other's have to expire. Delightful!"

Almost the instant the usurper spoke, the quality of the tormented woman's screams changed. Instead of the soul searing pain, the vocalizations dropped to a minor key and it was not so much a cry of terror as a challenging howl of bestial fury.

Ku'zn's green and amber eyes snapped open and she stared directly at Avael. Her growl became a roar. Before anyone could react, she grabbed the leg of the table holding the casket, swinging it to smash into the guards who still had their faces averted.

The Z'n snatched up a spear from one of the fallen men, and was suddenly running launched herself at the usurper with suicidal fury. The wall of troopers in front of the dais brought their spears up in an attempt to stop the Z'n, but the blue-furred warrior was a whirlwind of fur and fang.

Her bound hands did nothing to impede her skill with the spear that was so much like the traditional weapon of her people, the Z'n-K'Dar lance. She parried the thrusts of the guards and struck two of them down before they fully realized what had happened.

Ku'zn leapt past the guards to the platform where the nobles were screaming in panic amid the chaos, trying their best to get out of her way.

Bedlam exploded in the yard as the kneeling nobles, spurred equally by their own terror of the casket and their loyalty for Xull, turned on the usurper's guards.

At the same time, Xuxa, seeing her mentor battling to reach Avael, slipped her dagger from beneath her sleeping gown. Before the guard at her father's side could react to the unexpected act, the pre-teen stabbed him with all her might. The blade slipped in between the lacings of the soldier's corselet, just as Ku'zn had taught her.

The guard died instantly.

A second guard on the other side of her father made a grab for the girl but she dodged behind the king and sliced the bonds that held him.

Xull used the bar that had pinned his arms as a club, deflecting a sword thrust from the guard. Xuxa ran behind the soldier and slashed him behind the knee.

The soldier screamed and dropped to the ground just as the king brained him with the club.

Xull looked at his daughter as if to say, *Who taught you that?*

She looked to Ku'zn as he hugged her.

Ku'zn used her stolen spear as a scythe, cutting down the remaining guards before the usurper like wheat while moving up the dais to hack at the slower of the councilors.

Avael used his advisors like shields, throwing them in the path of the maddened Z'n who obligingly cut them down.

"I will give you half my kingdom," the usurper screamed. "My whole kingdom, just spare me!"

The blood rage of the Z'n could not be bargained with, however, and she growled louder as she cut her way to him. She sprang forward at the new king and thrust her spear into the usurper's gut, ripping up to drive it under his chin 'til it spitted his skull.

Avael's troops realized their leader and most of his advisers were dead, so many dropped their weapons to beg for mercy. There was no clemency in the shamed nobles, however, and they retaliated with gory justice, killing any of the traitor's men they could find.

Finally, Xull's commanding voice put a halt to the slaughter and loyal guards moved to surround him and his daughter.

Xuxa broke through the ring of soldiers to run to Ku'zn, stopping a dozen feet away from her with a gasp at the horrid sight the Z'n presented.

The blue furred warrior stood in the center of a circle of corpses, her fur matted with gore. Her eyes were narrowed into slits, her face fixed in a grimace and her breath coming in short, sharp growls.

"Ku'zn?" the princess whispered.

Gradually, the ragged breathing of the warrior settled to normal and she blinked to focus her eyes on the girl.

"Xuxa?" Ku'zn did her best to smile but was not very successful. The blood staining her teeth made her appear more frightening than friendly. Still, the girl ran to hug the warrior.

"I was so afraid," Xuxa said.

"Me too," the Z'n admitted.

The child looked up at her with a confused expression.

"But how come that fear box didn't work on you? I thought it worked on everyone's fear?"

"It did," Ku'zn said. "But the civilized fool did not realize that the Z'n people have only one fear." She looked up at the impaled usurper. Her smile became savage again. "And that is to die before we have slain our enemy."

Boys in the Basement
Jessica West

"SHE'S SCREWED EITHER WAY. You know that, right?" The old man leaned back just far enough to gain some momentum to launch himself out of the deep, wingback chair. These chairs were comfortable enough, and staples in any lawyer's office, but they were a bitch to get out of once the knees had reached a certain mileage. Mike's seemed to suddenly have had enough when he turned 60. "Wanna go for a smoke?"

The younger lawyer—not a young man himself, only by comparison, but considerably younger than his mentor—stared at nothing as he struggled to remove himself from the tangled mess in his mind. His elder patiently waited until Junior nodded and replied, "Yeah."

They moved outside to sit at a cast-iron bistro set in Junior's private patio, accessible only from the door in his office and completely surrounded by an eight-feet-tall privacy fence which did nothing to block the sounds of the street just beyond. The occasional passing car, rattling from the volume and bass of some rap song, drown out the noise of everyday life in a small town, Louisiana ghetto.

The small but sturdy chairs were much less comfortable than those inside the office, but Mike would gladly pay the price of a bit of discomfort while sitting in favor of struggling to stand up. The noise of the outside world was, unfortunately, a nuisance regardless of where they sat.

Mike offered the young man a cigar, but Junior, still not totally extracted from his thoughts, waved him off and lit a cigarette instead. The old man clipped the tip off one end of his cigar, rolled the thick length of it between his thumb and forefinger, then lit up. Smoky-sweet poison filled his lungs and relief flooded his brain. He waited while Junior worked through his client's predicament, coming to terms with it so he could properly defend her for murdering her boyfriend.

Sometimes, there is no right or wrong. Sometimes, you gotta make the choice you can live with. Sometimes, you pick the lesser of two evils. Everyone knows it. But knowing and accepting are two entirely different beasts.

"A mangled catch," Junior said.

The old man leaned forward in his chair. Junior and his metaphors had always fascinated him. "What's that, son?"

"When you catch a fish, reel it in, but the hook mangles the fish so badly that you know it won't survive. But you catch and release, and it don't pay to keep just one anyhow, so you toss it back like you're supposed to. She's a mangled catch."

Mike leaned back again to mull over his words, nodding to himself and watching the smoke drift between them.

City of Dry Creek
Parish of Avoyelles
State of Louisiana

Official Report

February 18, 2019

At approximately 17:45 on Monday, February 18, 2019, I (Officer Patrick Dupre) and my partner (Officer Jeremy Fontenot) was dispatched to 1911 Oak Street, Dry Creek, LA. Upon arrival, a woman later identified as Mya Ellis was waiting on the front porch steps. She said, "He's in the bathtub." She wouldn't say anything else. I told Officer Fontenot to stay with her while I went inside to check it out. I found the victim in a bathtub full of water and blood. I went back outside read the suspect her miranda rights and cuffed her and put her in the cruiser.

911 Transcript

February 18, 2019 16:38

Dispatch: 911, what's your emergency?

Caller: I need some help. My boyfriend bleeding. He won't go to the hospital. Oh God, please. *Unintelligible crying.*

Dispatch: I'm going to send someone to help you. What's your location, ma'am?

Caller: Unintelligible mumbling. 1911 Oak Street. PLEASE HURRY! He bleeding so bad. Oh God...*unintelligible screams.*

Dispatch: Someone's on the way now, ma'am. Is he breathing?

Caller: I told him get in the tub to stop the bleeding. The water supposed to stop the bleeding.

Dispatch: Someone's on the way. He'll be there soon. Just stay on the line with me.

Caller: ... [line disconnected]

Dispatch: Ma'am? Shit, I lost her.

Mike wondered if Junior wasn't better suited to some other career. The young man was brilliant, there was no doubt about that, but he felt things too deeply—contrary to what people believed. Junior was an expert at shoving all of those feelings down until it was safe to let them out. He'd take a hit, then space way out for a full second or two. When he "came back," he was different. Calm. Methodical. Completely emotionless.

Like now.

"So, you have a plan for your mangled catch?"

Junior tossed his cigarette on the ground and stamped it out. "Yep. Just gotta see which way she wants to go."

"What do you mean? She's gonna want out eventually, I'm sure." Mike leaned forward again, eager to hear the young man's logic.

"Why would she want out? She's safer in prison."

For all his brilliance in twisting the law to suit the needs of his clients, the young man didn't understand people. Not this unfeeling version of him anyway. Mike just shook his head and stood. "Well, let me know what she says."

"Will do. Thanks for coming by." They shook hands, then Mike left Junior to his work.

Avoyelles Parish Jail

Junior sat at a metal table, going over key words and phrases that he might use when defending Mya Ellis at trial. He couldn't make any solid choices yet, of course, but it helped to have the "boys in the basement"—a phrase he'd learned from some writing book he'd picked up about ten years ago—working on it. If he spent enough time focused on this case during his waking hours, his subconscious mind would provide all the answers he needed. It was almost like he had a literal team of Juniors in his mind, each with their own strengths, who worked together to make him more than he ever could have been on his own.

He was nine years old the first time he realized there was more than just his own voice in his head.

Someone had broken into their house one night when his dad was away at a conference. His mom had put Junior in the closet and told him to stay there no matter what happened.

The same closet where his dad kept a gun.

The man was beating his mother, and continued to do so even after he'd knocked her unconscious.

Her face looked like too much jelly spread over a slice of toast.

The whole room seemed to darken, then everything kind of went far away. The doors that were only inches away from his face a moment ago seemed suddenly beyond reach. A voice in his mind said, *I know you're scared, but if we don't do something, he's going to kill her.*

He couldn't remember anything that happened between that moment and the next, but he knew from reading the police reports that at least a few minutes had passed while he was *gone*.

During those minutes, he'd managed to climb the shelves in the bedroom closet, grab his dad's 9mm, load it, then rack the slide. He'd never been strong enough to do that, but his dad had showed him a trick where he basically slid the top of the gun against his jeans until it clicked. He'd learned plenty about gun safety, but hadn't yet made it to the shooting range for practice. Accuracy wasn't something he'd learned.

He killed the burglar and his mom that day.

According to the coroner's report, his mom was already dead before the first shot was fired. Blunt force trauma to the head. But guilt and grief are inseparable companions.

The metal door of the interrogation room opened with a loud screech as the corner dragged against the terrazzo floors. Detective Evelyn Bordelon escorted his client into the room, made the introductions, then left.

"Miss Ellis, I have some ideas of how to approach your defense but I need to know, first, whether you want out or if you'd rather stay in as long as possible."

"I... what?"

"I'm sorry. I meant, in prison. Do you want to be released as soon as possible? If so, I'm confident I can work out a plea deal. Your ADA is sympathetic. I could probably have you out on probation in a few years."

"My ADA?"

"Assistant District Attorney."

"Oh. Okay. Yeah, I guess I'll take a plea deal."

"Really? Okay, ah… I'll work on that angle then."

"Wait, did I have another choice?"

"We can fight the case, maintaining your innocence, and keep pushing back the court dates. That'd leave you in prison longer, where you're probably safer."

Fire lit the woman's eyes. "Why am I safer in prison?"

Junior backpedaled, completely unaware of where he'd gone wrong to make this woman angry. He didn't understand women at all.

"Won't the victim's family want revenge?"

A sneer twisted her lips. Apparently, she understood him much better than he did her. "I'll take my chances."

"She was screwed either way. You know that, right?" Mike sank into the wingback chair in Junior's office. He'd just smoked a cigar that morning, not half an hour ago, but already he wanted another. Anything to rid himself of the waves tension radiating off of Junior.

Junior nodded, that faraway looking coming back. He was shocked when he found out Mya Ellis had been killed in jail. After the shock wore off, he was just plain pissed.

"You can't take these things personally," Mike said.

"I know." Junior looked around his office as if seeing it for the first time. "You headed to the camp this weekend?"

"Course I am." It was opening day of squirrel season. Everyone was heading to their camps that weekend. "You're coming, right?"

"Yeah, I'll be there."

He wouldn't talk about the mangled catch. Not for a while. That was just his way. He'd deal with it on his own terms. Mike stayed long enough for the typical banter. He left safe in the knowledge that Junior would do as Junior always did. These things always changed him, but not necessarily for the worse in Mike's opinion.

The Ouija board Junior ordered just happened to come in that same day. His wife thought he was camping. Mike figured he'd changed his mind and stayed home. There was no reason for anyone to be alarmed. Not really. As heavily as that mangled catch had weighed on his mind, he kept it locked tight in there. No one had any reason to think there was any kind of problem at all.

Right about the time Junior got settled into his room with the board set up on his bed, I was booking Mya into Hell.

Oh, I know what you're thinking. But it's not that bad. Heaven is where the bland people go. The second circle of Hell is a form of Heaven for those lustful sinners. The seventh circle is for those who enjoy violence. Dante had it half right. You aren't punished for the life you chose to live. How you live your life is a good indication of where you'll end up, but it's more about where you fit in rather than how you'll be punished. Heaven and Hell isn't good or bad. Neither are people, for that matter.

You'll see.

Mya didn't really belong in any of the circles of Hell, except maybe Limbo, but she had too much fire for me to send her there.

"The fuck?" First words out of her mouth upon arrival.

I gave her the usual spiel, the same abbreviated version I've given you. We had better things to do.

Junior played with his Ouija board, and I brought Mya into his mind so we could watch. Well, so I could wait for her to adjust and him to go to sleep. I'm a nightmare demon, and while the cracks in his mind allow me to slip in, I can only really influence people when their subconscious minds are running the show. That's where I really shine.

When he stepped in front of the mirror to brush his teeth, that's when Mya fully realized we were in his mind.

"Take a look around you. What do you see, Mya?" Essentially, they always 'see' only darkness at first.

"Nothing." She wasn't freaking out, which was a great sign. I knew she had it in her. I can usually tell.

"That's normal. He'll turn the lights out and go to sleep. When he does, you'll be able to see more. Just wait."

"Okay..." Still wasn't freaking out. Even after the lights went out.

The lights inside his mind flickered, then dimmed, then finally came on full power. REM achieved. It wouldn't last long out in what people think of as the real world, but in here, I could make those moments stretch into eternity. It wouldn't take me that long to get Mya settled in.

"Tell me what you see now." The setting was different for everyone.

"A waiting room at the doctor's office where I brought my niece. Ain't no kids in here, though."

As soon as she said the words, the room came into view.

Along with its inhabitants.

"*Oh!*" Mya startled. "The hell?"

"These are... well, Junior calls them the boys in the basement. They're souls who've taken up residence here."

A tall man with a full beard and a roguish gleam in his eye turned our way. The teenage boy he was talking to when we entered sulked in the corner of the room as he approached. We probably interrupted whatever task Junior had set for the tall man that day before going to bed. Although he was torn up about what had happened to Mya, he had a whole slew of clients to try and save.

The tall man stuck his hand out for Mya to shake it, but she only cocked an eyebrow.

"Mya, this is Jeremy."

Jeremy lowered his hand but kept his expression friendly and open. This wasn't his first time welcoming a newcomer. "Pleased to meet you, Mya. I'm Junior's Protector."

"I guess you run things here?" She crossed her arms and settled into a fuck you pose. Full of fire, that one. Still, fire or no, she had to pass muster with the Protector if she was to stay.

"Not exactly. No one 'runs' things. But I am the only one strong enough to front, the only one Junior will defer to." His voice remained monotonous. He couldn't care less if she stayed or left. His sole purpose was to protect Junior. Nothing else really mattered. If she could be useful to him, he'd allow her to stay. If she posed a threat, even I couldn't force the issue.

She looked at me with that eyebrow still cocked. "What am I doing here?"

"When you died, one of your final thoughts was that you wished you could give that lawyer a piece of your mind."

She snorted. "Well, that ain't gonna happen."

Jeremy gave her a polite smile. "Not directly, no. But I could make that happen."

I could see the wheels in her mind turning. He'd never let her get to Junior, but there were other ways he could use her anger to make some improvements. It was all about perspective, and Jeremy was an expert at tweaking Junior's perspective.

"What's it gonna cost me?"

I had no doubt Mya would be an excellent addition to his collection. She was already negotiating the terms of her occupancy.

Junior woke with a start, rolled out of bed, and grabbed his cell phone. Mike answered on the third ring.

"Hey, Mike. You up?"

Mike chuckled. "Well, if I wasn't, I am now."

"I need you to lean on those two kids from the bus."

He'd never understand the way Junior's mind worked. He was sure the young lawyer was simply finding a way to cope with what happened to that Ellis woman. But he wasn't making much sense at all. Still, he'd give the young man the benefit of a doubt. He always had his reasons.

"Why? They were the ones who got beat up, Junior."

"Yeah, but they had to have been calling him names. Think about it. Two white boys. One black boy. No one on the bus yet. And they were all three sitting way in the back where the bus driver wouldn't hear. I'd be willing to bet they made some kind of racist remarks or something to get him riled up." He fell over trying to put his jeans on, so he put the phone on speaker and sat down.

"They caught him dead to rights, Junior. He's as guilty as they come. There's even video footage."

"Footage that conveniently can't be heard, only viewed."

"That's thin. And besides, wouldn't he have said something."

Junior hesitated only briefly. In that moment, Mike could almost see that calm, emotionless version of himself take over. "No, he wouldn't have said anything because no one would have believed him. It was his word against theirs, and you and I both know how that goes. But if they admit to flinging racial slurs at him... Mike, you're the best there is at getting people to talk. He's guilty of beating up those boys, but they were running their mouths for a full three minutes before he took the first swing. You saw the tape."

"Yeah." Mike nodded. "They probably had it coming. All right. I'll try to corner them today."

"Thanks, Mike."

Somewhere inside Junior's mind, he felt a deep satisfaction. The question of why his client had attacked those two boys had plagued him the day before, almost as much as Mya Ellis's death had. The answer seemed so obvious now that he'd put the boys in the basement to work on the case.

The Invader
Daniel Arthur Smith

EVAN SQUINTED AS HE made yet another attempt to solder-link the animatron's tiny circuit. Squinting didn't help. The circuit lay etched within a near transparent slate and the link-point was the size of a hair. "First go the eyes," he said. "Then goes the heart."

"What's that?" his daughter Nellie asked, her back reflecting in the animatron's oversized onyx eye. Her face was buried in her pocket vid.

"Something your Grandmother used to say. Kind of a tie-in response to *the eyes are the window of the heart*."

"I thought they were the *window to the soul*."

"That too," he said, squinting again in another attempt. "She believed…" He stopped mid-sentence to focus on the link point.

"Believed what?" asked Nellie.

"Hmm," he said, sitting back from the board. "She believed that love lit up the eyes and that, when love faded, the eyes went dull."

"I don't think so."

"No?" he said, perusing his tools. "You don't think there's a twinkle in the eyes when someone's in love?"

"Sure," said Nelly. "But that's not what you said."

"It isn't?" He picked up the thin laser pen and fixed its point over the target, then attempted to connect the tip of the arc pen again. The skeletal network of circuit surrounding the target glowed yellow, indicating a link.

"You said *first go the eyes, then goes the heart.* That's different than the heart fading *before* the eyes dull." She rocked back, rolling around on her backside to face him. Her cerulean eyes glowed iridescent in the reflection. "I think what it means is that you lose attraction, then fall out of love."

"Isn't that what I said?"

"No."

"Hmm. I suppose you're right."

"So, who's falling out of love?"

"Oh. No one," he said, applying a tester to the edge of the slate. "I was just having a hard time seeing something, and it made me think of that." A smile stretched across his face when the pathways of the etched circuit lit green.

"Ah," she said. "You meant *your* eyes aren't working."

"Yeah. I guess."

"I don't know why you insisted on uploading into that old syn skin in the first place."

"It's not old, it's age appropriate, just like yours."

"No. I mean one so old it doesn't have any tech. You could have at least gotten some implants."

"I have the neural lace just like everyone else."

"That doesn't count. How about an ocular implant? With augments and amplification to help you see."

"Then it's not authentic."

Her reflection in the large onyx eye mimed the word *authentic* as he said it.

"Hm," he said. "I guess *authentic* is a favorite buzzword of mine."

With a flip of her hair, she shrugged off being caught. "I wasn't mocking you," she said.

"No?"

"Maybe a little. More like mimicking."

"Mimicking?"

"Well. You point it out to me every chance you get. Your hover bike, *authentic,* our furniture, *authentic,* that thing you're working on right now for that four-legged animatron, the *vintage* listener, thingy—"

"Voice recognition system."

"Whatever," she pulled her hair back over her ear. "I'm sure it's *authentic.*"

"Okay, okay. So, I have an appreciation for nice things."

"Old things."

"Hey there," he scolded.

"I'm just sayin'," she said as she spun back around to face away. "When mother brought us to this colony, we had a whole wide catalog of synthetic shells to choose from. I mean, she's the Governor after all."

"Are we talking about my shell or yours?"

"I just don't know why I couldn't have my choice of shell. One I have to wear for who knows how long."

"But you did have a choice," he said.

"Of what mother said I could have."

"And what's wrong with that?"

"The only shells she let me choose from were young."

"Age appropriate."

"Whatever," she said. "I wanted something older."

"It's a bad thing to rush into maturity."

"That's exactly what she said."

"And she was right. You should hold on to sixteen for as long as you can. Besides, when your birth body arrives on the *Somnium Sleeper* ship, you'll be a closer match."

"I know, I know. But I have to wear this one for who knows how long."

"I know. And so do you. Two more years. Besides, your friends Delilah and Jesse, don't they have the same aged syns?"

"Well, Jesse does. I think Delilah's getting an upgrade."

"She told you that? I can't believe her mother would approve."

"She was called out of class the other day and I haven't seen her since. Ms. Bliss said she's visiting her grandmother off-world, but Jessie and I think she's getting an upgrade."

Nellie was quiet for a long moment, then spun back around toward him.

"Dad?" she asked.

"Yes," he said. He slid the repaired circuit slate into the side of the animatron's barrel belly.

"Have you ever had a dream about something you were sure was real?"

"Yeah, sure. I think everybody has those."

"No." She shook her head. "I didn't say it right. I mean a dream that stays with you even after you wake up."

"You mean you remember it?"

"No. I mean that you dream something, but when you wake up you still believe it's true. Like reality."

"Huh," he veered his focus up towards the analog clock his wife had hung high up on the kitchen wall. The minutes lit a neon blue as the glowing second-hand ticked past. He counted five, then answered. "No. I don't think I've ever had that happen."

"You're sure?"

"Uh…Yes. I'm sure."

When Nellie didn't reply, Evan looked at her reflection in the onyx eye. She was sucking her lips into her mouth, something she did when she was stressed. So, he swung around to face her. "Is something bothering you?"

She smirked then said, "You'll think it's silly."

"Probably," he said, prompting her to smile. "Go for it anyway."

"Well. There's this girl."

"One of your friends?"

"No. I haven't met her before."

"Okay. Someone from the vids."

"No." She shook her head again. "It's not like that. This girl—Emily is her name—she started showing up in my dreams."

"And?"

"Now she's showing up when I'm awake."

"You mean you're hearing voices?"

"No, no. That would be crazy. I mean I hear her in my dreams, but when I wake up, it's like…it's like she's still with me. It's like I feel her presence the same way as I do in the dream."

"In the dreams where she talks to you?"

"Uhuh," Nellie nodded. "What do you think it means?"

"I don't know what that means," he said. With a grin, he added, "But I don't think you're crazy."

Evan tossed his toothbrush back onto the little toiletry mat to the side of the sink. He swished a mouthful of water to rinse, spat it out, then reached for the light switch. But before he flipped it, he caught his reflection in the mirror and, thinking about what Nellie had said, leaned in to examine his eyes.

He tightened them, widened them, then turned his face slightly side to side.

The inspection revealed that the flesh below his eyes was a bit puffy—he hadn't been getting enough sleep—but apart from the subtly glowing blue tint of the neural lace behind his orbs, they appeared normal.

He smirked for doubting himself, flipped off the light, then went into the bedroom where Harper was already waiting under the covers, swiping her fingers across a small vid screen.

"Still haven't picked one out?" he asked.

"I just don't know what I want to wear," she said. "I don't feel like I'd look good in any of these."

He laid down beside her and reached over. "Let me have a look."

She handed him the vid then he too began to swipe. "No. No. No. Oh. Here. This would look great on you." He handed the vid back.

"That's a cocktail dress."

"Is it? What's wrong with that?"

"It's too short."

"You look good in short dresses."

"Thank you. But I'm a mother and the Governor."

"Who looks good in short dresses."

"I'll wear one for you, Dear, but not for the gala. I'll look again tomorrow when I'm fresh." She set the vid down onto her nightstand then touched the shade of her lamp to dim the light.

Evan stared up toward the ceiling. "I was talking to Nellie earlier," he said.

"She's still upset about her shell?"

"As a matter of fact, she is."

"She'll get over it. I was the same way at her age. It's part of growing up."

"Yeah. Of course. You're right. But that's not what I wanted to tell you."

"What then?" she asked.

"She said she's hearing voices," said Evan.

"Oh. Emily? Yeah. She told me about her."

Evan turned to face Harper. "You don't think that's strange?"

"An imaginary friend? Some kids get them."

"At sixteen? Again, you don't think that's strange?"

"I'm sure it's a coping mechanism. She was uprooted midway through high school, and she's the Governor's daughter. That makes her life a little...complicated. She's coping."

"I suppose you're right. Maybe she should talk to somebody."

"That would probably just make things worse."

"Okay. But if it keeps up—"

"If it makes you feel better, I can have Larissa check in on her."

Evan rolled onto his side and placed his hand on her shoulder. "I'd like that," he said, then leaned close and kissed her neck.

Harper placed her hand over his then squeezed. "I have to be up early," she said.

With a sigh, Evan rolled onto his back, pulled the top pillow from beneath his head, tossed it to the floor, then readjusted himself and closed his eyes.

Evan found himself standing in a short corridor, a hallway with a white wall to the right and a glass wall lining the left, outside of which towered the chromium spires of New Dunedin and the red dwarf sun of Gliese 667C and her two sisters. At the end of the hall was a single door—the number nine dash forty-one printed on the designation plaque to the side.

The faint whisper of a man filled his head. *Open the door.*

Evan darted his head side to side. He was alone.

The voice repeated, *Open the door.*

He slowly spun around; but there was no one.

The third time the voice spoke louder, tersely and determined, *Open the door.*

Then, in a raised voice, the man spoke from directly behind. "*Open the—*"

Evan spun toward the voice, but before he could identify the speaker—

He woke to the beep of his alarm.

Images of the hallway played over in Evan's mind as he dressed: the cityscape, the door, the voice. *Open the door.* He didn't taste the toast and jam Harper had left for him. The walk to his hover bike was a blur, and as he entered the commuter path to the city center, the voice traveled with him.

Open the door.

A messenger drone merged onto the path before him, inches in front of his hover bike. Evan was caught off guard, but instinct kicked in. Unfortunately, he squeezed too tightly on the brake, jerked the handlebars to the right, and sent the back of the bike into a swerve off the path, plowing sideways into a crowded walkway. Screams rang out as pedestrians dove out of his way.

The scooter came to an abrupt stop and Evan nearly flew off.

He held tight as the bike wobbled to a sturdy position.

A man in an all-black suit stepped toward him. "Hey, Barry," he said. "Is that you?"

Evan looked at the stranger, shook his head, then launched the hover bike back onto the path, switching over to autopilot for the rest of the ride—something he rarely ever did.

The rest of the morning was the same: the hallway, the door, and the voice continued to haunt Evan, not so distant, not a memory, more like a presence, the way Nellie had described.

Open the door.

The speaker was with him somehow.

Midway through a planning meeting, New Dunedin's librarian Peter Lang, seated by his side, had to loudly clear his throat to bring Evan to attention.

Ruth Mansfield, the commerce commissioner, was seated across the table. "Evan?" she said. "Are you here with us or somewhere else?"

"What?" said Evan. "Yes. Of course. I'm right here with you."

"Then what say you?" she asked.

Evan smiled apologetically. "I'm sorry."

Ruth sighed deeply, then continued. "We're discussing Stanford Silicon and the syndicate's lack of payment since the conflict began in the Cervantes system."

"Well," said Evan, "as I understand, negotiations are ongoing."

"The issue at hand," said Ruth, "is that lack of sponsorship for New Dunedin's Stanford Silicon contingent is a drain on the colony."

"Yeah. But that's just paper."

"Paper?" Ruth's brow furrowed.

"You know," said Evan. "It's not real, it's a construct for alloca—"

"I assure you," Ruth said sternly, "the allocation of resources is very real."

"She's right," Peter said in the calm fashion of his ilk. "Construct or not, until we're fully sustainable to trade with the other syndicates, our allocation system is credit based. Credits that come from sponsorship."

"That's how you see it?" asked Evan.

It was then that Elaine Potswaith, representative of the Company, spoke up. "It is how the Company sees it," she said. In New Dunedin, the Company's viewpoint weighed heavily; after all, their syndicate had built the colony.

Jasper Maguin, representative to the council from the Mining Consortium, added, "The Consortium considers it a bargaining chip if the policy is continued."

Ruth tilted her head to the side. "You do agree with the shared stance of the Company and the Consortium?"

"Yes," said Evan. "Of course. But shouldn't we run this by the governor?"

Ruth smiled. Peter rested back in his chair.

"What?" asked Evan.

"It's her recommendation," said Ruth. "She added it to the agenda."

"I see," said Evan.

"Then it's settled," said Ruth. "Colonial members of Stanford Silicon will continue to be put on ice until the conflict is resolved and sponsorship resumes."

Evan nodded. In truth, he couldn't put his head around the politics of the moment, not while a voice was whispering into his ear, *"Open the door."*

That night, Evan returned to the glass walled corridor and door nine dash forty-one.

Again, he heard the man's voice.

Open the door.

"Who are you?" asked Evan. "What do you want?"

As if to mock him, the voice simply replied. *"Open the door."*

But this time, the voice was clear, familiar, and right next to him.

Evan spun to the source of the sound.

His jaw dropped. His heart stopped.

Standing before him was him, his mirror image, stern-faced and eyes burning blue.

The second Evan leaned forward, inches from Evan's face, then spoke again. *"Open the door."*

Eyes half open, hair muddled, Evan dressed then went to the kitchen to eat.

His toast waited for him at the counter as it did each morning, two halved slices, with a small jar of jam and a cup of fresh juice from the colony's Botanical parked to the side. He took a seat at his stool then, staring into kitchen, began to eat the toast dry.

He chewed through his first slice slowly, laboriously, and it was only when he reached for the cup of juice that he realized Nellie was seated at the table.

Her eyes were sunken, her face gaunt, her long hair uncombed, and in her hand was a spoon at rest in a full bowl of oatmeal.

"Shouldn't you be in school?" he asked.

"I wasn't feeling well," she said. "I didn't sleep."

"Still having dreams about Emily?"

She nodded yes.

"How about the door with the number nine dash forty-one?"

Nellie's eyes widened. "How do you know about the door?" she asked. "Are you seeing it too? Is Emily talking to you? I knew this was something. I'm not going crazy."

"Yes. No."

"What does that mean?" she asked.

"Yes to seeing the door. No to seeing Emily."

"The door's real then. Do you know where it's at?"

"No," he said. "Not exactly. But I'm going to find out."

He reached into his pocket, pulled out his vid card, then rapidly typed a message to Peter Lang, the New Dunedin Librarian.

Peter, odd question, can you do a search? I'm looking for a door designated 9-41. I know it's in a building in the east quadrant.

Peter immediately responded.

"Huh," said Evan.

"What?" asked Nellie.

"I messaged Peter Lang. He says he knows the location, and to meet him at the Archive."

"When?"

"He wants me to stop by at noon."

"That's incredible. Can I come?"

"No. I'm going to head to work. Why don't you lie down? I'll get to the bottom of this."

Evan arrived at the Archive center to find Peter waiting in the lobby.

The Librarian greeted him with a smile. "Good morning," he said.

"Good morning," echoed Evan. "Thanks for meeting me."

"It's quite all right." After a short pause, he said, "Are you okay? Excuse me for saying, but you look a bit rough."

"Yeah," said Evan. "I've been having some trouble sleeping."

"Oh," said Peter. "That makes sense."

"Makes sense?"

"It will. Anyway, I'm glad you reached out."

"You know about the door then?"

"Yeah. Sure," said Peter. He pointed to the floor. "It's here in the Archive. The ninth level actually. Jen-Five should be along any minute. The ninth level is her domain. She'll accompany us down there."

"Jen-Five? The synthetic caretaker?"

"Yes. In fact, there she is now." Peter stepped over to greet Jen-Five as she crossed the lobby, then rejoined Evan. "Evan," he said. "You remember Jen-Five."

"Certainly," said Evan. "Jen handled our transfer from the *Somnium Six*. Hello."

Jen-Five had short blond hair and iridescent blue eyes that appeared to glow brighter than the pale blue of her jumpsuit. Her caretaker attire was a bit out of place with the fashion of those passing by, but her smile was warm and her voice calm and relaxed. "Hello Mister Harbin," she said. "How've you been?"

Evan cleared his throat to sound stronger than he was. "Well, thank you."

"I've seen the Governor on the vid-stream. She seems to have hit the ground running."

"Yes. Indeed," he agreed. "That's Harper."

"I understand you wish to inspect the ninth level?"

"If you don't mind."

"Not at all," said Jen-Five. "I'll take you down there now."

Evan said nothing as Jen-Five led the two through the lobby and into a lift. As the lift accelerated downward, the back wall of the shaft disappeared to reveal the chromium towers outside of the Archive, an image captured from cameras high above. Evan stepped toward the full wall-screen. "Huh," he said. "The image. It's what I saw."

"What you saw?" asked Jen-Five.

Evan caught himself. "Nothing," he said. With a ping, the doors of the lift slid open, saving him from any further explanation.

The Caretaker led them into the corridor. Evan took two steps then froze. His breath went short and his forehead dampened with cool sweat. The presence was heavy, overwhelming. This was where the dream occurred. The white wall to the right, the chromium towers to the left, another image from above, and before him, a door—door number nine dash forty-one.

A lump seized his throat as the Caretaker reached for the handle then opened the door.

Jen-Five and Peter began to enter the dark room then stopped at the threshold and looked back at Evan still near the lift.

"Are you coming?" asked Jen-Five.

Short of breath, Evan nodded and *eeped* out a weak, "Yeah." He forced a smile, inhaled deeply, then followed them into the room.

The room beyond the door was a black void. Evan stopped just inside as Jen-Five disappeared into the darkness. Silently, a long row of glass faced cryo-tubes lit up one-by-one before him in a rapid cascade—fifty pods deep. When the last of the aisle lit, another row of pods facing the first lit up in the same cascading manner and when that the row finished, the process repeated in the level above, then one above that, and then one more— four levels high, a catwalk ran the length of each.

Jen-Five led them down the aisle to the right. As they passed, row after row, level after level of stacked cryo-tubes lit up on their left.

"It's like a Somnium ship," said Evan.

"On a smaller scale," said Jen-Five. "We've only ten thousand cryo-tubes in this facility."

"They appear to be occupied."

"Just short of half."

"And they're all syns?"

"Goodness no," she said. "The incubators are in the industrial gardens. These are all sleepers,"

"Sleepers?" said Evan. "I didn't realize..."

"It's a standard storage system," said Peter. "Think of it as the New Dunedin version of the Lions Meadow."

At this, Jen-Five proudly looked back and smiled.

Evan nodded. Having grown up on Titan, the Lions Meadow was a place he'd never been, but every school child learned of it early. It was a vast underground facility back on Earth containing the birth bodies of countless early colonists who cast themselves out from the Homeland into the stars via neural lace, in the same fashion he and his family were cast to New Dunedin when their birth bodies went into the *Somnium Six*. But something didn't add up.

"I thought the facility was for catastrophic emergencies," said Evan.

"In initial intent," said Peter. "Turns out, it's also a peaceful means to dealing with a conflict situation."

"You mean," Evan asked, "These are all—"

"Members of Stanford Silicon," said Peter.

Jen-Five stopped and turned to face them. "You were aware?" she asked. "Isn't that the purpose of the inspection."

"Of course," he said. "Seeing it in person is just…" He shrugged. "I didn't imagine there were so many."

"The protocol was ongoing when your family arrived," said Peter.

"For how long?"

"Quite some time," said Jen-Five. "Would you care to see some of the new intakes?"

"Yes," said Evan. "That sounds good."

"Right this way," she said, leading them into the adjacent aisle. As she walked, she gestured toward the occupied pods. "The row to the left," she said, "are Stanford Silicon colonists stored in the last cycle. Those to your right are the current intakes."

She continued talking, but Evan had tuned her out, again overcome with the presence of his mirror self. Absently, he scanned the faces as they passed, men, women, teens, children—none he recognized, though some he thought he did, then he came upon a familiar face.

"Delilah," he said, stopping before the cryo-tube.

The Caretaker stopped her tour and spun around. "You know this young woman?"

"Yes," he said. "She's a friend of my daughter. I thought she was a syn."

"No. That's her birth body."

"She's visiting someone, isn't she?" he asked. "Someone off-world, a relative maybe?"

"No," said Jen-Five. "That's something we tell the younger people and those who inquire about a whereabouts or change."

"Change?"

Peter interrupted, "It's another allocation optimization."

"I don't understand," said Evan.

"The bodies," said Peter. "Well, they're in fine health. They make suitable short-term hosts for visitors and newcomers. No need to waste a full-cost synthetic shell."

"You mean, you place other consciousnesses into these people? Without their consent?"

"We do have their consent," said Jen-Five. "It's in the charter."

"How many people know about this?" asked Evan.

"It's not necessarily a secret," said Peter. "More of a *need to know.*"

"What about their consciousness? If they're not off-world, then where are they?"

"They're in there," said Jen-Five.

Evan frowned. "Aren't they backed up to the Archive?"

"Sure," she said. "There's a copy made during the storage procedure. But they aren't wiped. They're left to dream."

"Like the sleeper ships," he said.

"Very much so, at least until a new consciousness is loaded into their neural lace."

"Thank you, Jen-Five," said Peter. "If you don't mind, Mister Harbin and I are going to chat for a bit. If you could make the arrangements we discussed?"

Jen-Five smiled widely. "If you need anything, just call." She then turned and walked away.

"Evan," continued Peter, "when you asked about the door, I thought it was important to bring you here. I'm guessing you've been out of sorts. You already said you're losing sleep."

"I have been," said Evan. "So has my daughter. I think there are some issues with our syn shells. It's becoming apparent to me what the source of the problem is."

"And what do you think it is?"

"It's clear to me that this shell was obviously in use before I was cast into it, and that it most likely wasn't wiped, just like our friends here—that's the reason for the residual—echoes if you will."

"Yes. It's quite possible that, as the two of you were processed simultaneously, that's the cause of what you and your daughter are experiencing. There's more to it, though."

"And what is that?"

"I think you know the answer," said Peter. "Think about it. What did Jen-Five say about syns when you brought them up?"

"That they were in the industrial gardens."

"That's right. What does that tell you?"

"If Jen-Five is the caretaker of this facility, why was she assigned to place my family?"

"Think about it."

Evan paused for a long moment as the pieces came together. "This syn I was cast into, it isn't a syn at all, is it?"

Peter shook his head.

"It's not a synthetic shell, it's human. It's the body of a colonist, a member of Stanford Silicon."

"That's right."

"My wife? My daughter?"

"Your wife seems to be fine. Your daughter, however, appeared to be suffering the same anomaly."

"Appeared?" asked Evan. "You've seen her?"

"The Governor—your wife—brought Nellie in for a reset this morning. Right now, Jen-Five is prepping a tube for you. She'll temporarily pull you from this body, reset the neural lace, then reinsert your consciousness. You shouldn't have any more visions or visits in your dreams."

"The other presence," said Evan. "You knew about that too."

"Like I said," said Peter, "it's rare, but it happens."

"The other presence I've been sensing...He's this body's original owner." Evan held his hands up and stretched his fingers wide in wonder. "I'm the invader."

ABOUT THE AUTHORS

Steven Van Patten is from Fort Greene, Brooklyn. After graduating from Long Island University on a full-tuition scholarship, he pursued a career in television production. After paying his dues, Steven went on to stage manage a plethora of TV shows, most recently *The Mel Robbins Show* and *The View*, all the while dreaming up his macabre tales. The storyline of his first novel was born from watching horror movies as a child and noticing a lack of diversity, and character development when people of color were employed. After pouring over historical research night after night, and traveling alone to various locales, including Senegal, West Africa and Osaka, Japan, he wrote the first three installments of the ***Brookwater's Curse*** horror novel series, which featured a 1860s Georgia plantation slave who becomes a vampire.
After receiving much praise, several glowing reviews from various book club heavy hitters, and literary awards for each book, Steven was admitted into the Horror Writer's Association. His next two novels, *'Killer Genius: She Kills Because She Cares'* and *'Killer Genius 2: Attack of The Gym Rats*—pitted a hyper-intelligent, socially conscious female serial killer against a well-intentioned African-American detective. It debuted at NYC Comic Con in October of 2015 and was nominated for an *African-American Literary Show Award* for Best Mystery/ Suspense in 2016. Three years later, *'Hell At The Way Station'*, Steven's collaboration with Marc Abbott, a horror anthology with a sort of Arabian Knights twist, won Best Anthology and Best In Sci-Free.
Visit Steven at his website: https://brookwaterscurse.com

Amy Grech has sold over 100 stories to various anthologies and magazines including: *A New York State of Fright, Apex Magazine, Beat to a Pulp: Hardboiled, Dead Harvest, Deadman's Tome Campfire Tales Book Two, Expiration Date, Fright Mare, Hell's Heart, Hell's Highway, Needle Magazine, Psycho Holiday, Real American Horror, Tales from The Lake Vol. 3, Thriller Magazine,* and many others. *New Pulp Press* published her book of noir stories, *Rage and Redemption in Alphabet City.*

She is an Active Member of the Horror Writers Association and the International Thriller Writers who lives in Brooklyn.

Visit Amy at her website: www.crimsonscreams.com

Follow Amy on Twitter: twitter.com/amy_grech

Teel James Glenn was born in Brooklyn and has traveled the world for thirty years as a Stuntman/ Fight choreographer/ Swordmaster, Jouster, Book Illustrator, Storyteller, Bodyguard and Actor (Yes he was Vega in Streetfighter: the later Years). And has done over 80 films and 55 Renaissance Faires in most of the above capacities.

He's had stories and articles printed in scores of magazines from *AfterburnSF*, *Classic Pulp Fiction stories*, *Blazing Adventures*, *Weird Tales*, and *Mad to Black Belt and Fantasy Tales* and a number of books published.

You can keep up with his new adventures at: theurbanswashbuckler.com

or his blog: theurbanswashbuckler.blogspot.com

Jessica West (a.k.a. West1Jess) is currently pursuing a state of self-induced psychosis, also known as writing. In the past, she has worked for Wal-Mart, a lawyer, and a bank. Now if she could just get a couple years experience with the IRS and the NSA, world domination is in the bag.

Jess lives in Acadiana with three daughters still young enough to think she's cool and a husband who knows better but likes her anyway.

For news and updates visit west1jess.com

Daniel Arthur Smith is a USA Today bestselling author. His titles include *Spectral Shift, Hugh Howey Lives, The Cathari Treasure, The Somali Deception*, and a few other novels and short stories. He also curates the phenomenal short fiction series *Tales from the Canyons of the Damned* and *Frontiers of Speculative Fiction*.

He was raised in Michigan and graduated from Western Michigan University where he studied philosophy, with focus on cognitive science, meta-physics, and comparative religion. He began his career as a bartender, barista, poetry house proprietor, teacher, and then became a technologist and futurist for the Fortune 100 across the Americas and Europe.

Daniel has traveled to over 300 cities in 22 countries, residing in Los Angeles, Kalamazoo, Prague, Crete, and now writes in Manhattan where he lives with his wife and young sons.

For news and updates visit danielarthursmith.com

Made in the USA
Coppell, TX
20 April 2021

54183851R00059